John Farman

THE SHORT AND BLOODY HISTORY OF HIGHWAYMEN

Red Fox

A Red Fox Book

Published by Random House Children's Books
20 Vauxhall Bridge Road, London SW1V 2SA

A division of The Random House Group Ltd
London Melbourne Sydney Auckland
Johannesburg and agencies throughout the world

Copyright © John Farman 2000

1 3 5 7 9 10 8 6 4 2

First published in Great Britain by
Red Fox Children's Books 2000

Printed and bound in Great Britain by
The Guernsey Press Co. Ltd, Guernsey, Channel Islands

Papers used by Random House Group Ltd are natural,
recyclable products made from wood grown in sustainable forests.
The manufacturing processes conform to the
environmental regulations of the country of origins.

The Random House Group Limited Reg. No. 954009

www.randomhouse.co.uk

ISBN 0 09 940711 6

CONTENTS

WHO, WHAT AND WHERE WERE HIGHWAYMEN?

It's a dark, moonless night about three hundred years ago. There you are, riding home from the theatre, minding your own business, when out of the shadows comes a lone rider with a small mask and a bloomin' great pistol demanding your money or your life. What sort of a bloke would do that, I sincerely hope you want to know?

If you've read the first book in this series (the one about pirates), you will have realised that the sort of chap that went in for plundering on the high seas was almost always from the lower orders of society. Also, he was almost always a bit short in the old education department (in other words as thick as two short planks). In fact you could count those who could read or write on one hand (if you could count).

Posher Than Pirates

The highwayman was very different. Okay, when push comes to shove, he did do more or less the same sort of thing – rob people – but this time on a horse rather than in a boat. Much more interesting, I think, is the fact that many of the highwaymen were gentlemen from rather distinguished backgrounds. And, even if they weren't, they certainly made out that they were (if you see what I mean).

Quite a few of these highway robbers had been born into dead flash homes and had therefore been brought up proper-like (like your dear selves). Despite these early advantages they had seen it all go severely pear-shaped at some stage or other. Some had been chucked out of the family home for inappropriate behaviour (sometimes with inappropriate chambermaids), while others had been left out of a will on the death of a rich daddy or uncle. William Parsons, for instance, had a father who was a baronet and an aunt who was a proper duchess. Poor Bill went to Eton school, was expelled, gambled away his fortune, took to the road and ended up his illustrious career swinging from the gallows at Tyburn. So far as we know, he was the only ex-Etonian to go into the highway robbery business.

Blown the Lot

Others had received their inheritance but had simply blown the whole caboodle in a feast of loose living or had chucked it away at the many gambling establishments in Georgian

England (1740–1830). So, what really connected them was that they were all broke, overdrawn, bankrupt, skint, potless or whatever you want to call it, and all faced the terrifying prospect of having to earn an honest living like everyone else. They couldn't even claim social injustice as an excuse.

Now these guys couldn't be seen to be doing a proper job, like you and me*, so in order to live in the style to which they'd become accustomed, the robbing of those who'd managed to hang onto their wealth was the only avenue open to them.

When?

The Golden Age of the highwayman in England and Scotland was most definitely between 1700 and 1800.

How?

Simple! It was all down to the roads – or, should I say, the lack of roads. There had been practically none built since the brilliant Romans had visited some 1200 years before. These days, we nonchalantly slide the car or bike out of the drive onto a neatly tarmacked street and are able to get to wherever we want to go on similar interconnecting roads and carriageways.

Can you imagine a time when even the equivalents of our motorways were nothing more than broad tracks through fields, almost impassable in the sopping wet, muddy

---

* *Writing this stuff, a proper job – who am I kidding?*

winters and almost as impassable in the summers when the same deeply rutted roads would be baked hard like overdone pizzas?

Not only that, but the population in the seventeenth century was still only around 6,000,000 which meant there were wide expanses of deserted forests and common land with just a few well-worn tracks across them. There was only the merest fraction of houses along these roads – never mind all the ghastly service stations which we now have up and down the motorways. Travellers over two hundred years ago could plod along for hours and hours on end without passing any sign of another living soul. Add that to no street lighting and the fact that the coaches moved at a snail's pace (fast snails admittedly) and would break down at the drop of an axle, and you have the perfect hunting ground for the notorious 'gentlemen of the road'.

Others

There were, of course, other sorts of men who became highwaymen. Many had been soldiers during the English Civil War (1642–1649) but, when the armies were disbanded, they found themselves on the point of starvation, miles from home, and without any prospect of earning an honest day's wages. The real peak was between 1697 and 1701 when a load of unemployed, disillusioned and thoroughly desperate soldiers returned from the wars with France.

Other highwaymen held perfectly respectable jobs, but used them as a cover for their night-time activities. William Davis, a smallholder born in Wrexham (page 81), for instance, was called the 'Golden Farmer' because nobody could understand how he could have become so rich from farming. Likewise John Cottington (page 77) was a chimney-sweep by day and a robber by night (at least he didn't have to black up!).

By the Way

Many of the would-be highwaymen actually hired their first horse rather than risk being caught aboard a stolen animal. They usually bought their own after their first major payoff.

How Often?

Don't, like I did, go thinking that robberies by highwaymen were relatively few and far between. On the contrary. It appears that it was rare *not* to be bushwhacked or at least chased and threatened if you journeyed any great distance across England's green and pleasant land during the golden age of highwaymen. As one much robbed and weary traveller put it, 'highwaymen are as common as crows'. As for crossing London, many wealthy gentlefolk employed a

special servant (often armed) to accompany them and hopefully discourage the footpads (unmounted robbers) who seemed to lurk in every alleyway.

What's Coming?

But let's talk about the book that you're about to read (this one I hope). How, you might ask, will it be any different from all the other stuff you can read about highwaymen? Well I'll tell you. In this mighty volume (what I'm about to write) not only will I describe the naughty comings and goings of most of the famous and not so famous highwaymen (and women) but, in addition, and this is much more fun, I'll attempt to let you in on what it was actually like to be one – on a day to day basis: the upsides and, much more to the point, the downsides of life as a lone robber on the open highways and byways of England.

BUTCHERS UNITE

If you go through the records of the execution of
highwaymen at Tyburn, you'll notice that, apart from the ex-
toffs and soldiers mentioned in the last few pages, there seem
to be far more ex-butchers than those of any other profession
who were hanged as highwaymen. This may seem a bit weird
at first – I mean, can you see the connection between meat
and highway robbery (apart from it being so expensive)?

At the end of the seventeenth century, butchers saw
themselves as a slight cut* above the common hordes and
were regarded by all as ever so respectable (not to mention
well-off) professionals. But, as the century lumbered on, your
ordinary butcher lost this reputation, for reasons I will explain,
and started to associate with the more criminal elements (a bit
like some second-hand car salesmen these days).

So what were these reasons? For a start, being in the dead
animal business, so to speak, butchers were well aware of the
value of the beasts that travelled to and from the
countryside. In fact, meat, in its various forms, either
waddled, plodded, shuffled or skipped its way along every
muddy road into London (and to meet its maker).

* *Bad joke!*

More to the point, the animals' owners always returned the same way, usually themselves slaughtered (from drink), having swapped their charges for hard, jingly cash.

Big Business

Meat, by the way, was very much the staple diet of the British in those days and, because of that, the amount and quality that a man could put on his family's table was a clear indication of how well he was doing — in other words, it was a status symbol. Hardly anyone grew vegetables in those

days, unless desperately poor, and anything that came out of the ground (apart from bread) wasn't really regarded as proper food. Meat was far and away the biggest business going and was traded amongst the beer-swilling and tobacco-smoke-swirling taverns like the Rose and Crown, The Swan with Two Necks, The Bear and Ragged Staff or the Golden Lion that were concentrated in and around the ancient Smithfield meat market in the centre of London.

It would not be going too far to say, in fact, that meat, in its various forms, was the hub around which all commerce revolved. It influenced the amount of forest land which had to be cut down to provide pasture (a bit like major burger bars do now), and the number of tollgates set up to maintain the hoof-trashed roads. And of course, in a still entirely agricultural land, the meat trade was an enormous source of employment.

But the whole of the meat business had become awfully corrupt by the early 1700s, with sub-quality, sometimes dangerously 'off' cuts being sold on the unregulated and often criminal market by unscrupulous 'jobbers'. It got so bad that a lot of the respectable butchers and poulterers (and all the little businesses that relied on them) really began to feel the pinch.

Wits' End

Being mostly husbands and fathers and mostly middle-aged, butchers dreaded losing their families and their homes, so much so that many of these men, at their wits' end, were forced to look for other ways of making money when their trade went belly up. It didn't take long to work out that a bit of light highway robbery would help to restock their ailing businesses and that their inside knowledge of how the meat business worked (and how and when the cash moved around) would lead them to their prey. James Dalton, for instance, an ex-master butcher fallen on hard times, was caught and convicted of highway robbery three times, three times transported, and three times returned to London, before being hanged (once!) in 1730. Not to mention the most famous highwayman of all, Dick Turpin, who was also apprenticed as a butcher and even had his own shop before launching into his new, much more profitable career.

Top Baddies

Finally, it must be said that highway robbery was regarded among the common folk as almost respectable – it was certainly the most romantic and exciting way of committing a crime. Let's face it, if you were poor, robbing smart people in smart coaches meant nothing to you. If anything, highwaymen were thought of as Robin Hood-like characters – instead of being hated by the public (as were pirates and thief-takers), they were seen as heroic figures, and the stories of their lives and dastardly doings were swapped and enjoyed by everyone (even those who got robbed). There was very little shame in the early seventeenth century in being recognised as a highwayman.

OF COURSE WE WERE ROBBED BY CLAUDE DUVAL

All Together

But it wasn't just the butchers who'd been suffering. All the little people who surrounded the meat trade – the small-time dealers in herbs, eggs, poultry and butter – were having a hard time as well and actually encouraged the highwaymen to go about their business. Innkeepers and cook-house owners were in on the act too, keeping a sneaky eye on the drovers and graziers on their way back from market carrying lots of lovely gold and silver. They were quite happy to give their highwaymen friends the nod now and again.

Daniel Defoe, top writer of the time (Robinson Crusoe, etc.), tipped off travellers of any description to keep their distance from the innkeepers or ostlers and to be careful about how much they said to strangers, either in the inns or on the road. Even the turnpike men and gatekeepers were caught between loyalty to their old friends (the highwaymen) and the law which was beginning to breathe down their necks.

SUPPERTIME IN HIGHWAYMAN-LAND

On the whole, highwaymen were lonely sorts of blokes (just like writers) and were usually as solitary off-duty as when they were at work. Because they were nearly always on the run from the law, they only carried the sort of possessions they could get on the backside of a horse. Consequently few had proper homes with proper wives to go to, sleeping where (and with) whomever they could. They would lodge in inns and taverns and either have food (etc.) sent up or they'd patronise the various eating-houses and cookhouses which were so much part of the English scene in the seventeenth and eighteenth centuries. Highwaymen, by the way, were dead popular with the more dishonest owners of the taverns and eating-houses, as they were usually pretty free with their ill-gotten loot.

By the Way

In the eighteenth century, London employed over 35,000 people in its eating and drinking establishments (the population as a whole still hadn't reached a million) and it was one of the only trades which those born poor could enter and stand any chance of bettering themselves.

Thieves' Kitchens

If, however, your off-duty highwayman needed to fence some of the hot gear he'd just nicked, he could trot down to the local thieves' kitchen. These secret establishments, like gambling and opium dens, catered for all the local low-life. The quality of the food and drink they offered bore a great resemblance to the clientele – rough and extremely tasteless. It must be said, you'll be pleased to hear, that most of our self-respecting 'gentlemen of the road' saw themselves as a cut above that sort of thing and wouldn't dream of associating with the likes of common burglars, pickpockets and cut-purses. They were regarded as the elite of the underworld.

As I say, on page 35, most highwaymen lived in or around London, so, rather like these days, finding stuff to eat really late in the evening was no problem.

Restaurants

Restaurants were, as you can probably guess, a French idea (on account of its being a French word), but in England, way back in the eighteenth century, there were hardly any as we know them today (with long menus, poncy waiters and the like). Everyday eating houses in Restoration England would seldom offer you a choice of food (just like your mum doesn't). Indeed, if you ate out, you took the meal of the day – called 'the ordinary' – like it or lump it (again, just like home).

Having said that, London and some of the bigger cities had whole streets of cookhouses all offering something slightly different. These rough-and-ready, family-run establishments mostly catered for people whose humble lodgings★ had no facilities for home cooking. The alternative was for the residents of the poorer houses to take their own pies and tarts and put them in the nearest baker's always-hot oven for a nominal fee (this happened well into this century in some poorer areas).

By the Way

It's thought that the term 'cockney' comes from the people who owned and ran the thousands of London cookhouses.

Takeaways?

Don't go thinking that takeaways are a new idea. All the cookhouses did a take-out service even in those days – they had to. Eating out, or simply buying your meals out, was more of a necessity than a luxury if you were anything short of rich. Even our poor old highwayman might well have sent a boy out for something to eat when he got home cold and tired after an especially hard night's robbing. Alternatively, once he'd parked, fed and tucked up his horse, he could buy something off the street from the many street vendors. Stuff like eels, oysters, pies (or oyster pies), black puddings or cakes and penny custards.

★ *Most people rented in those days.*

How Much?

In the few more up-market places (where the better-off went) the average cost for a good meal would be around five shillings, which might seem a bit of a bargain but, translated into today's money, would be around £18.00 – not cheap in a society where most of the people lived on practically nothing. In the more down-to-earth establishments the charge would be far less.

In the cookhouses, the actual cooking would often be done in the same room as you ate. It would noisy, full of steam and tobacco smoke with a large piece of dead animal turning relentlessly on a spit at one end, powered by either a child of the family or sometimes the family dog in a sort of treadmill. This treadmill would be set on the wall and the poor pooch (known as the turnspit dog) would never stop, having to relieve himself as he best he could as he carried on running (pee while you work). Health and safety regulations? – I don't think so. There'd be a big cauldron bubbling over the fire containing a sort of never-ending stew, and every now and again semi-edible objects, sometimes of a very dubious nature, would be chucked into it. Vegetables, which had for centuries been the staple diet of the poor, were at that time rather unfashionable (because they had been the staple diet of the poor) but many who could not afford much meat still ate a sort of porridge, made of peas, to fill them up.

How Offal

Nothing was wasted. People in those days often ate bits of animals that we wouldn't go near, let alone eat! Grisly stuff like calf's head and feet, umble pie made from the 'umbles' (entrails) of venison, sheep's head and feet, ling's fin (a sort of fish), tripe (sheep's stomach), cows' udders and ox's cheeks. And – just to make you go really straight – a real delicacy would be to boil up into a continuous stew all those nasty odds and ends like lips and ears and noses (and much worse!*) that we throw away (or put in pork pies or dog food). Apologies if you're a bit squeamish (or a veggie).

Fancy a Drink?

The one thing you could be sure of was that highwaymen never drank water when back in the city. Come to that nobody else did in those days. The reason was simple – it was filthy to the point of being poisonous (and so would you be if you'd just come out of a river which all the sewage had been chucked into). Nor did they drink cow's milk because they thought it too was unsafe, which it probably was. Oddly enough ass's milk was popular for the sick or for young children and the lady asses (lassies?) were dragged round the streets of the bigger cities and milked on the spot.

Beer for All

The truth is, everyone drank beer – mums, dads, grannies, maiden aunts, clergymen – even school-kids. In fact the boys

---

* *Use your imagination.*

21

at Eton, the poshest public school of all, were punished if they couldn't drink their daily allowance (try me, try me – I hear you cry). There was 'small' beer which was fairly weak and 'strong' beer which most certainly wasn't – and it was all dead cheap.

As for highwaymen, they loved to drink and get drunk on strong drink and they loved the places where strong drink was drunk. They were famous for their often very rude drinking songs. Some took the mickey out of thief-takers and constables, some celebrated the love of women (to put it delicately), some were about the meat trade (see page 13), some about the exploits of fellow highwaymen and their love of the open road, and some simply glorifying drinking and getting totally pi . . . pie-eyed. Their most favourite drinking song went like this:

> Now we are arriv'd to the Boozing-Ken [maybe an Inn],
> And our Pockets full of Cole [money?];
> We pass for the best of Gentlemen,
> When over a flowing Bowl
> Our Hearts are at ease,
> We kiss who we please;

On Death it's a Folly to think;
May he hang in a Noose,
That this Health will refuse,
Which I am now going to drink.

Highwaymen awaiting trial in Newgate (see page 47), like in many other prisons, were usually not short of hard 'rhino' (the underworld term for money) and could buy liquor whenever they wanted from the gaoler (who had usually taken a degree in corruption). There was a deadly tipple called 'South Sea' and a wicked gin that was made on the premises, called at various times 'Cock-my-Cap', 'Kill Grief', 'Meat and Drink' or simply 'Comfort'.

WHAT TO WEAR?

One of the highwaymen's (or highwaywomen's) greatest probs was knowing what to put on when they went about their shady business. For a start they couldn't put on their everyday clothes, or they'd be recognised right away. And they certainly couldn't wear anything too flashy, or bright coloured, as they'd be spotted instantly while lurking in the gloom. And they couldn't wear what they wore for 'work' when they came home in the morning, for obvious reasons. So what were they supposed to do?

In the late seventeenth and eighteenth century, there was to all intents and purposes a sort of uniform for highwayrobbers – a full-length, black embroidered jacket, silk waistcoat, tight buckskin breeches, a white shirt with a cravat at the neck, black leather shoes with big shiny buckles or tall leather boots with brown fold-over tops – the outfit of an extremely wealthy country gentleman in fact. On his head he would wear the obligatory three-cornered hat edged with gold braid and underneath he'd have what we would regard as a rather poncy powdered periwig tied at the back with an even more poncy bow. He would own lots of these wigs – all, of course, a different colour from his own hair for obvious reasons. False beards go without saying, but some highwaymen stuffed the ends of their wigs into their mouths to help hide their appearance. Most importantly, he would wear a black mask over his eyes and sometimes a silk hankie round his mouth – he couldn't take any chances.

Some highwaymen, like the infamous, Gamaliel Ratsey (great name – eh!) who was hanged in 1605, wore a nasty-looking hood, with a nasty-looking face painted on it, covering his own – nasty-looking face.

Did You Know

That the saying 'to pull the wool over someone's eyes' dates from this period? As wealthy men of the period wore wigs, highwaymen would often pull a victim's wig over his eyes so that he couldn't see who was robbing him.

Men as Women

Then there were the disguises. James Collett did his robbing dressed as a bishop, with his partners in crime dressed as his chaplain and servers, while Thomas Sympson was one of a number of cross-dressers, passing as a rather passable woman.

A bit too passable as it happens. On one occasion, West Country highwayman Sympson, while riding in a coach with a well-known peer of the realm, was looking particularly fetching, so much so that the peer made a sly pass at him (an occupational hazard methinks). Our Tom said (no doubt in his highest voice) that he would prefer to be seduced away from the other passengers and so saying led the peer into the woods. On lifting Tom's voluminous petticoats the naughty old peer noticed that this

gorgeous damsel (later known as 'Old Mob') was wearing a pair of men's breeches which he found somewhat off-putting to say the least. On his questioning Tom about these trousers, the highwayman replied that they were to put all the peer's money in and he then proceeded to hold him up. Needless to say our hero didn't hang around to be seduced.

By the Way

Sympson later robbed Judge Jeffreys, the notorious hanging judge and one time Lord Chief Justice of England. This wasn't a good career move, as he ended his days in 1691 at Tyburn, swinging around in front of his adoring but heartbroken wife, five kids and countless grandchildren.

Women as Men

There were a few highwaywomen and they mostly dressed as men, which made it easier to ride horses (no skirts involved) and much simpler to cover their identity when they slipped back into their normal lives as women. The most famous was Mary Frith, who was born around 1584 and, to be honest, was a bit butch to start with. I mean, how many women do you know who have a violent temper, carry a sword, smoke a pipe and drink themselves silly every night in lowdown taverns? Your mum! Oh dear, I do hope I haven't put my foot in it.

Moll Cutpurse

Cobbler's daughter Mary started out as a simple pickpocket and purse-snatcher in and around the streets of London, and she was known as Moll Cutpurse throughout the teeming underworld. She was even branded on the hand with a red-hot iron – a popular way of marking small-time thieves in those days. At 60 she thought that she'd go into the big-time and went on the open road as a highwaywoman during the Civil War, having loads of fun robbing the Roundheads with her friends such as Royalist Captain James Hind (see page 57).

Mary had always been aware of the pittance that she was given by the fences (dealers in stolen goods) compared to the value of the stuff she stole, so decided to go into the receiving business herself. She soon became one of the very biggest and best receivers of stolen goods and made a fortune. So much so that she eventually lived in a massive house with lots of servants and, despite her spectacular ugliness, had loads of lovers of both sexes, and lined her mansion wall-to-wall with mirrors.

But bad old Mary couldn't give up 'the road' and she was eventually caught, tried, and sentenced to death. But by this time, as you can imagine, she was so rich that she was able to buy a pardon for £2,000 (about £132,000 now) – a massive fortune in those days. It seems a bit outrageous to think that if you had enough money in olden times, you could get yourself out of practically anything.* 'He cannot be hung who hath Five Hundred Pounds at his command' wrote highwayman Francis Jackson.

* *That's something only politicians seem to be able to do these days.*

By the Way

Mary obviously had a great sense of the ridiculous – even near the end. She requested, while on her death bed, aged 75, that she be buried bottom upwards so that she could be as preposterous in the afterlife as she had been in the first one. My kind of woman.

Barecheeked Robbery

There was one highwayman who didn't worry a bit about clothes – he simply didn't wear any. One of the famous Cherhill gang, who terrorised the Bath Road, used to leap out on his unsuspecting victims wearing the same outfit he was born in, waving a gun (and everything else presumably). Apparently it scared them into parting with all they had on them.

TRAVELLERS' TRICKS

As robbery on the king's or queen's highways reached fever pitch, the ladies and gentlemen who were being robbed began to suss out the situation and developed loads of smart ways to avoid losing their money or their lives (or their wives).

Armed and Dangerous

There was a big market for dear little flintlock pistols in the seventeenth century – small enough to be hidden in a pocket, or down a ladies front, or in the muff that ladies often used to keep their hands warm. One of the major drawbacks to this was that the firing mechanism was always on the outside and the bloomin' things were likely to go off at a mere sneeze. Talk about shooting yourself in the foot!

Half Robbed

A great stunt to avoid losing your often not-very-hard-earned money was to cut all your bank notes in two. You could then carry half with you and send the rest on later. In those days, you could simply stick the two bits together at a later date and carry on as normal. The trouble with this was that it often miffed the highwayman so much that he shot the clever person dead – out of spite. This sort of ruined the point of the exercise.

All I've Got

Most people would try the oldest trick in the book, which was to carry a fairly small amount of money in an obvious place, and hide the rest in a less obvious place. This was all very well, but highwaymen weren't stupid and they threatened to duff up the victim if they did find any more than they were expecting (especially if they looked rich). Others had their suits or frocks made with hidden pockets, or used specially designed foot warmers with extra pockets for money and jewellery.

Home-Sewn

Probably the most ingenious were the women who sewed coins into the very linings of their clothes. This was all very well but, if your highwayman got wind of this, he was likely to take the whole frock and leave the ladies somewhat embarrassed (not to mention chilly).

Shooting Back

Best of all was to travel with armed guards, and many wealthy people chose their servants according to how handy they were with a gun or sword. It was not uncommon, therefore, to have a bit of a shoot-out on your journey, especially if there was a gang involved.

Not a Sniff

Quite a good wheeze was to hide valuables in something that was rather foul-smelling, like over-ripe cheeses or pungent ointments (or old socks). This was fine if you could put up with the smell for your whole journey.

Protection Money

Some highwaymen found a way of earning money without even leaving the tavern. Regular travellers would pay them regular money NOT to be robbed when out and about. Not only that but the villains would ensure that nobody else robbed their 'patrons' while they were on their particular patch – a kind of early protection racket. There was one super-cheeky villain called Whitney, self-styled the 'King of the Highwaymen'. He presented a proposal to the government in which he offered to keep the roads clear of his fellow felons for £8,000 a year. They naturally declined his kind suggestion.

Not Well Pleased

Although the more refined highwaymen showed little violence towards their chosen victims, others really lost it big time, especially if they thought they were being cheated. These horrid chaps had generally started their criminal careers as common footpads (street muggers) and were certainly of a different class to our gentlemen of the road. For a start their language was less than polite and they were known to fling terrible insults, most of them unprintable – but some just about: 'You suffocated dogs in doublets', 'You spawn of hell hatched by Beelzebub' or even 'You double-poxed long-arsed salivated bitch in grain' (and they're just the nice ones!)

One rather unpleasant character, Irishman Patrick Fleming, was accused of having murdered five men, two women and a fourteen-year-old boy. Not only that but he'd cut off the ears, nose and lips of a man who'd had the bottle to resist him.

There was also a particularly unpleasant character from Bedford called Jacob Halsey who, amongst a string of

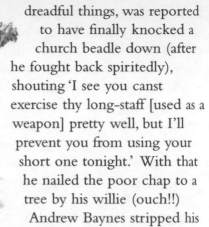

dreadful things, was reported to have finally knocked a church beadle down (after he fought back spiritedly), shouting 'I see you canst exercise thy long-staff [used as a weapon] pretty well, but I'll prevent you from using your short one tonight.' With that he nailed the poor chap to a tree by his willie (ouch!!)

Andrew Baynes stripped his victims if they claimed they had nothing on them and would then thrash them with his riding-crop if he found they'd been hiding anything. On one occasion a woman, while being robbed by the vicious highwayman, swallowed a very valuable ring, presumably with the idea of retrieving it later (if you get my meaning). He was, understandably, rather cross and, without further ado, slit her open, retrieved the ring, and then filled the poor woman's tummy with stones (odd?) leaving her dead by the roadside.

Another, John Withers, forgot to put his mask on one day (silly chap) while robbing a postman. To avoid an embarrassing encounter at a later date, he cut the poor postie's throat, sliced open his stomach, filled him (also) with stones and then chucked him into a river (which makes more sense if you ask me).

On another occasion a poor woman struggled to remove her diamond wedding ring while being held up by the impatient brute. The poor dear ended up losing her finger as well.

Gilder Roy, a Scotsman from a very fine family, (Rob Roy?) got most pleasure from killing those who put up the least fight (unfair or what?). He once held up a judge who didn't much like the idea of parting with the jewels he was carrying. This annoyed Gilder who proceeded to strip the coachmen and footmen, tie them up tight and then chuck them into a pond where they all perished. He then hacked the coach to pieces, shot the horses (shame!) and hanged the old judge for good measure.

The Royal Mail

In the olden days much more was moved around the country by the ordinary mail, especially hard cash, and with no railways or planes it had to go by road. In the seventeenth and eighteenth centuries it was carried by a single rider on a single horse. These brave post boys would ride between the inns which acted as depots for the mail. A single man on a lonely road (inns were usually about ten miles apart) was, as you might imagine, a sitting target for highwaymen. The problem got so bad that huge rewards were offered to anyone who could track the highwaymen down. The Post Office, founded 1649, tried everything to keep the post safe, by using strong metal boxes or fully armoured coaches but, right up to the end of the eighteenth century, nothing proved robber-proof. The answer, as always, was to put their hands even deeper in their pockets and spend more money, which they did in 1784. The result was a series of new super-fast mail coaches smothered in smart Royal Mail livery and drawn by four super-fit horses. These had a driver and a guard who sat alone on the mailbox armed with a blunderbuss (a nasty weapon which shot a lot of little lead balls in a wide arc which meant that the shooter didn't have to be that accurate).

The new coaches would tear around the country, free from toll charges, with the driver blowing a long post horn to warn the guards to open the turnpike gates as they approached. Few of these coaches were ever successfully robbed.

By the Way

These tollhouses often held large amounts of money if the road had been particularly busy, and they were a favourite source of loot for the old highwayman. The penalty for any interference with the tollhouses, was death by hanging and no messing.

REASONS TO BE WARY

If you went down to the woods in the seventeenth or eighteenth centuries you'd be sure of a big surprise – and not from teddy bears. Areas such as forests were especially dangerous if travelling long ago. Also, as I mentioned in the introduction, the terrible state of the roads had much to do with the speed at which coaches could travel (and the ease with which the highwayman could stop 'em).

Quite a large percentage of highwaymen chose to live in or around London for fairly obvious reasons. Firstly because it was by far the biggest city in England, so it was easy to get lost among the throng of people that practically lived on the streets of London in the 1700s. Secondly, London turned into countryside and woodlands the moment you left the city (no suburbs in those days). Thirdly, because there were no proper banks: most of the big money tended to move in and out of the city by road and, best of all (if you were a robber), in gold and silver. Lastly, the valuable stuff that wasn't gold or silver had to be got rid of (or fenced), and in London there was a network of Fagin-like fences – faceless men who could convert any thing that wasn't cash ... into cash.

Bad Roads

If you were carrying a lot of money, travelling along some particular roads was like putting your head in a lion's mouth and hoping for the best. They were a magnet for highwaymen.

The Dover Road

The road that ran from Dover to London (now the A2) was always dodgy to say the least, right back from the early 1500s. Gads Hill was always popular with robbers as it was near Chatham from where the freshly paid sailors travelled on their way to London to spend their hard-earned cash. Shooters Hill in Woolwich was also treacherous - hence the name. In 1797 a post-chaise carrying a couple of lawyers and a midshipman from the HMS *Venerable* was stopped on Shooters Hill and the passengers severely beaten, with pistols being forced into their mouths. The poor sailor lost all his clothes when they stole his trunk.

By the Way

Highwaymen always attacked on hills (upward) because their victims would be sure to be travelling far more slowly.

The Bull Inn, Shooters Hill (particularly steep and dangerous) was a famous coaching stop in those days and the first post drop-off on the road out of London. Here highwaymen like Dick Turpin would lurk to see who was going where and when and, more importantly, – with what. Beside the Eltham Road, which crossed it, was a line of gibbets (places to hang people after they'd already been hanged). Samuel Pepys noted in his famous diary that, one day in 1661, on his way to Dover, he 'travelled right under the man that hangs upon Shooters Hill, and a filthy sight it is to see how the flesh is shrunk on his bones'.

By the Way

Coach drivers often suffered from drowsiness which was something to do with the rocking motion of the vehicle and something to do with the amount they drank at the coach houses. It was not unusual for a highwayman to leap out and be practically run down by the galloping horses whose driver had fallen fast asleep.

The Bath Road

Despite Bath's reputation as an elegant and genteel city, there was nothing elegant and genteel about the road you had to take to get there. The A4, as it is now, was alive with brigands anxious to rob wealthy travellers on their way to take the famous mineral waters. An ad in the *London Gazette* of December 1st 1681 offered a reward of ten pounds plus expenses for information leading to the arrest of the highwaymen who held up a Mr Joseph Bullock on the road between Hungerford and Newbury. The ad listed the rather insignificant goods stolen from Mr Bullock and, at the end, casually mentioned the murder of his servant, John Thomas, as if it were little more than an inconvenience (which it probably was).

Hounslow Heath

The Bath Road crossed the notorious Hounslow Heath (now hemmed in between urban sprawl and a loud airport), which was crawling with highwaymen. It was also crossed by the Exeter Road (A30) and this crossroad was a prime site for villains like the notorious French villain Claude Duval (1643–1670) looking for rich pickings. More unusual was a local highwayman called Twysden, who, legend has it, turned out to be the Bishop of Raphoe in Donegal. He was shot dead while at work on Hounslow Heath. (The Lord moves in mysterious ways).

Another lord, The Fifth Earl of Berkeley, had a massive stately pile at Hounslow (now probably a housing estate) and was robbed so many times that he used to go everywhere armed to the teeth. He killed quite a few highwaymen in his time including Cran Jones who was burned to a cinder when his clothes were set alight by one of the Earl's better close-range shots.

The Great North Road

There was only one man that you can truly link with the A1 or great North Road and that was Dick Turpin. His innumerable robberies were mostly carried out in the Finchley area, now a rather gloomy suburb of London. Finchley Common, another favourite hanging location was risky until well into the 1800s.

The Oxford Road

These days, on the road going north-westish out of London towards Oxford, the countryside starts around Hillingdon. In the seventeenth century Hillingdon was where journeys began to get a bit safer, as it was too far away for the highwaymen to travel to. But once you reached Shotover Hill, Oxford, the bad lads were usually waiting to jump out on travellers who thought they'd almost made it.

The West Country

I don't know about you, but I still wouldn't feel that safe crossing Salisbury Plain at night on a horse (you'd probably be mown down by army patrols and druids). In the eighteenth century, it was about as daft a thing as you could do. The West Country had always been a favourite haunt for highwaymen.

Knightsbridge

Practically the worst thing that can happen to you in Kensington, these days, is to be accosted by some old biddy asking the way to Harrods, or being solicited for change for a parking meter (with or without menaces). In the 1700s it was very different. Right up to 1798 highwaymen hung around Knightsbridge, robbing coaches that got stuck in the mud caused by the streams that then ran from Hyde Park. It got so bad that, for a time, a bell would ring at intervals on a Sunday evening to attract those people returning to the City of London who didn't care, or dare, to travel alone. They would only set off when they had a sufficient number to put off the robbers.

North Out of London

If you go out of London via the A11 (to Newmarket,

Cambridge etc.) stop a minute to consider how lucky you are compared with those of days gone by. The Newmarket Road was so dangerous that in 1617 there was a hand-to-hand battle between highwaymen and irate locals. Five of the crooks were injured and at least one killed. Nearer to London, a bunch of recently exed soldiers, desperate to find something to do, formed a sort of highwayman's co-operative in Epping Forest. They became so successful that in the end the Lord Chief Justice was forced to send a detachment of dragoons to ask them (not very nicely) to desist. All they did, however, was to scatter and reform elsewhere.

Did You Know?

One of the reasons we drive on the left in England dates back to these times. A coach driver being usually right-handed preferred his assailant to approach from the right either in a carriage or on horseback so that he'd have his sword-arm nearest. Highwaymen, of course, soon got wise to this and would lurk on the nearside – out of range of a flailing blade.

TRADE SECRETS

I don't suppose that knowing how to spot highwaymen really holds much interest these days. I mean, some shady guy wearing a three-cornered hat and a mask, waiting on horseback at the corner of your street, might seem just a little obvious, especially if you live somewhere like Hounslow★. But in the mid-eighteenth century, highwaymen were much more difficult to spot.

Francis Jackson (alias Dixie the Highwayman) was the first in a long line of English highwaymen who sold their stories to entertain the public. Not only that, but when he'd hung up his own robber's outfit, he gave out information on the tricks of his trade and also how the general public could go about spotting his ex-partners in crime (cheeky and not a little dangerous, I should imagine). First of all, here is his advice for anyone contemplating a life on the open road (with a bit more of mine thrown in).

★ *Hounslow, now a London suburb, was once a favourite highwayman's haunt.*

41

Tips for the Would be Highwayman

1   Never stay in any one lodging for any length of time and be sure to have a variety of false names at your command (that goes for writers as well).

2   In your lodgings keep a selection of wigs, false beards, patches and anything to disguise your appearance. When actually out robbing, it's a good idea to put a pebble★, or some such thing into your mouth to change the sound of your voice.

3   Have your own personal watchword or phrase, like 'What's a-clock?' or 'What shall we have for supper?' As soon as you say this, grab the victim's bridle, shove your pistol in his face (accompanied by a torrent of swear words), and, with a bit of luck, he should deliver the goods instantly (heavily confused I should imagine).

4   If your victim's horse is faster, fresher (or prettier) than yours, do not hesitate to exchange it (or take both). But beware, it could be identified later so it might be worth carrying the wherewithal to disguise it (like something to colour-in any white bits).

5   Make your victim swear, on pain of a bullet in the brain, not to follow you or raise the alarm.

6   Always cut the girth and bridle of your victim's horse so that he can't chase after you.

7   When returning late from a night's work, muffle the sound of your horse's hooves by placing woollen stockings over them.

★ *Editor's Note: This is a tip for highwaymen and should not be tried at home.*

8   If attacking a group, travel slowly on the road and let
     them catch up with you. Single out the one who looks
     the wealthiest and engage him in pleasant chit-chat. If he
     doesn't know his fellow travellers, suggest that they're a
     bad lot and probably out to rob him. Once you have
     fallen a few hundred yards behind the others, pull out
     your pistol and hold him up. Even better, have some
     mates hiding in the bushes and ask them to hold you
     both up. Tell your new friend that they are bound to
     shoot you both if you don't stand and deliver and so
     saying give the robbers (your mates) your money. Your
     new friend will almost certainly do the same. Finally
     when your chums gallop off, tell your fellow victim that
     you are sure you know which way the gang are going
     and point the other way.

9   If you are ever caught and find yourself in court, have a
     story ready that will make the jurors weep with pity: –
     you know, impoverished family – dead parents – little
     brothers and sisters starving – stealing solely to feed
     them – ever so sorry – never do it again etc. etc.

10   Why not try this? Arrive reasonably near to your proposed
     place of ambush, in a perfectly normal four-wheel open
     carriage with two horses. Change into your highwayman's
     outfit and unhitch one of the horses to do the robbery
     on. When finished, return to reharness the horse, change
     back into your normal clothes and drive home, innocent
     as the day is long, as if nothing had ever happened.

11   If the goods stolen are too recognisable to fence
     (exchange for money) in England, take them across the
     channel, especially to Holland where there's a ready
     market for diamonds and jewellery.

12   Avoid mail coaches. They're too heavily armed and
     you'll be bound to swing if caught.

Having said all this, many of these tricks of the trade mentioned above were frowned on by proper 'gentlemen of the road', they preferred to rely on simply a horse, a pistol and a quiet bit of road. Highwaymen were supposed to be 'honest thieves' and would never be seen using such low-down common trickery. Oh yeah! – and my name's Dick Turpin!

Tips for Travellers (in the seventeenth century)

Jackson gave this advice for anyone contemplating taking valuables on a journey.

1   If carrying money, never tell anyone how much. Trust no one.

2   Never say when or where you're going, or even say goodbye to anyone. Always try to slip away undetected.

3   Never travel on Sunday (the most dangerous day), as the roads are quieter and the highwayman stands less chance of being disturbed. Also the county authorities will do nothing to help, as the Sunday Trading Act relieves them from the responsibility of reimbursing you if you get done over.

4   Beware of any stranger who sidles alongside and tries to have a chat. If someone does, keep changing pace – even stopping. If your new would-be chum follows

suit, you know you're in big trouble.

5   Try not to travel alone: there's safety in numbers.

6   Don't rely on the 'silly, old decreeped men' (as Jackson described them) employed as watchmen along the way at places where robberies have occurred. At any sign of trouble they are more than likely to run (or hobble) as fast and as far away as possible.

7   Always say your prayers (and make your will) before setting off on a long journey.

Tips for Honest Innkeepers (few and far between)

The few respectable innkeepers acted as informants to the Bow Street Runners and the thief-takers.

1   Keep a wary eye on anyone who seems rather inquisitive either about a fellow traveller – or about his horse, where he's going or what time he's leaving.

2   Get the ostler to examine a suspect's saddle bags to see if they're empty. If they are, this means they're simply for show (and so that his horse can go that bit faster).

3   When showing someone suspicious to their room, ask the servant to remain outside for a couple of seconds to see if she can hear the jingling of coins. If the door's got a peep-hole – so much the better.

4   Get various people in your employ to ask a suspect's name. If he makes up a new name every day he'll probably trip over himself.

5   At suppertime, tiptoe to the man's room and rap furiously at the door to tell him it's ready. If you hear scuffling, or things falling over, or stuff being quickly stuffed away – you know for sure he's up to no good.

6   If your suspect's hanging around during the day time and spots someone riding by who looks rich or is

carrying interesting looking baggage, see if they jump up and claim he's a beloved relation or friend that they simply must speak to – a sure sign.

Tips for Crooked Innkeepers

1   Tell your trusted staff to be alert for particularly heavy baggage. It will probably contain coins.
2   Keep an eye out for money carriers, especially those transporting cash collected as taxes.

By the Way

On one occasion, a heavily escorted carrier was robbed of £15,000-worth of tax money while travelling from Manchester to London. The thieves obviously weren't horse-lovers, as they stabbed to death sixteen of them, so preventing the thieves being followed.

CAUGHT GOOD AND PROPER

It's a bit of a sad fact, but most highwaymen spent their very last days in prison. So what, I expect you think! Prison life ain't so bad. Well, maybe not now (tellies in every cell etc.), but prisons in those days, I'm afraid to report, were rough, tough, miserable, horribly overcrowded and no fun whatsoever. Mind you, if you still had enough money, you could pay for a lot of the little comforts that make life bearable – but we'll go into that later.

The most infamous and most typical of all these prisons was called Newgate. The word alone sent shivers up the spine of anyone who'd done anything remotely naughty in eighteenth-century London. If you want to know where it was, take a tube to Ludgate Circus and walk down Fleet Street to the Old Bailey. It was first built on that site in 1218 and was only demolished (almost unbelievably) early in the twentieth century.

The Castle of Newgate (as it was nicknamed) was divided into three bits, one for men prisoners (that's where most of the highwaymen went), one for the ladies and another for people who owed money.

By the Way

If a debtor had less than ten pounds in the world and had no hope of paying back his debt (and there was no fraud involved), he could be let out. But, if the person to whom he owed money insisted, he could be kept in prison as long as that person paid his eighteen pence a week keep.

Between these three sections were the keeper's house, lodgings for the turnkeys (as the gaolers were called), a chapel, a press room (coming later), condemned cells and, best of all, a taproom (bar), where gaolers and visitors (or prisoners with money) could buy booze and tobacco. There was also an unofficial viewing gallery where the public could come and gawp at those poor beggars condemned to death. The gaoler would charge an admission fee for this treat. For example, despite the unbelievable stench of the Condemned Hold (as it was called), thousands of visitors in 1724, pressing vinegar-soaked hankies (bad enough, I'd have thought) to their noses, filed past the miserable highwayman Jack Shephard as he lay manacled and chained to the floor waiting to meet his end.

On the other hand, although chained up in their own private condemned cells, some wealthy highwaymen could still entertain visitors, right up until they were taken to Tyburn. William Hawkes, 'the Flying Highwayman', received many lords and landed gentry, charming them with his ready wit, while awaiting execution in 1744.

By the Way

Some highwaymen like Frenchman Claude Duval (see page 72), became massive sex symbols to upper-class women – a bit like rock or film stars. Many of their blokes (including the aristocracy), you see, were unmanly to the point of effeminacy and the ladies swooned at the tales of the highwaymen's daring deeds.

No Go Area

But Newgate, through most of its history, was so filthy and disease ridden that even the rats thought twice about moving in. It's said that the atmosphere was so dodgy (it stank to high heaven, actually) that visitors were known to faint just breathing it in. Even the water, which came from a spring, was joined by the overflow from the cesspool – a heady cocktail. Jail fever, the collective word for typhus, typhoid and lots of other nastiness, did for more of the condemned than the actual gallows. This might also have been because doctors refused to go anywhere near the place. And nor did anyone else, for that matter, for it used to be a great laugh for the prisoners, if they could reach, to pee and/or empty their chamber pots out of the windows onto the passers-by, and for the most disgusting oaths to issue from the underground women's quarters, from gratings just beside the pavement. All in all, Newgate was not somewhere you'd want to go for your holidays.

By the Way

The head keeper for each of the prisons would pay £8,000 for the job. He would make a huge profit on the deal, by charging all the gaolers, who would, in turn, extract cash from the prisoners.

Torture for All

I mentioned the 'press room'. This wasn't, as the name suggests, somewhere the local newspapers came to get the latest criminal gossip – it was a place for pressing information or confessions out of anyone they thought was telling porkies. Highwaymen would be pressed for information about their accomplices or where they'd stashed their loot. Heavy weights (25 stones-worth) were placed on a door and then placed on the strapped-down 'client's' chest. So far so bad. Then, after half an hour of this, one by one, extra weights were added until either:

a) the poor devil confessed all or even lied just to get the weights off or

b) the victim died an excruciating death with a crushed chest – the air being literally squeezed out of him. This awful treatment wasn't abolished until 1792.

Newgate had all the normal old stuff like whipping-blocks and the pillory. The pillory, in those days, was an interesting form of rough justice that I really do suggest you don't try at home with your little brothers or sisters (or pets). The prisoner was held in a standing position in a contraption like the old-fashioned village stocks and the general public would be invited to throw things at him or (her) – which was fair enough. If the mob weren't too bothered, they'd simply chuck stuff like squashy fruit, old veg and rotten eggs etc. and this was usually the end of it – home to a warm bath and bed. But if the public were really cross, they'd throw dead dogs and cats (and their respective muck), rocks, stones or anything they could lay their hands on. It was not unknown for prisoners to be bludgeoned to death by this method.

By the Way

Sometimes the poor victim was nailed by his ear to the pillory, and was often required to leave the ear (and the other one) behind, when his time was up.

Almost worse than all this, some Newgate residents who hadn't done anything quite bad enough to be hanged, were left, literally, to rot to death, manacled to their cell floors. If they had just a little cash they could bribe their keepers into an 'easement of irons', but this would only last until the gaoler reckoned the money had run out, a bit like a parking meter – well . . . a bit!

Not Bad

Despite all this misery, at certain times in Newgate's history there was often a lighter side, in fact in some respects it was quite a laugh (but only if you had money). With only one gaoler to ninety prisoners (it's about one to six these days), discipline was lax to say the least. For the right bribe, wives could stay overnight, children could live in, pets and pigs and poultry could be kept (until 1792), newspapers could be delivered, naughty ladies could seek out clients, and at one stage there was even a sort of gymnasium area where the cramped prisoners could stretch their limbs. There were sometimes wild and very wicked parties, free from a lot of the restrictions that might have existed outside.

HOW TO HANG A HIGHWAYMAN

Strange as it might seem, hardly any of the better known highwaymen managed to avoid being dragged up before the law. It's all very well using the disguises and stuff I've already mentioned, but if you start bragging about your exploits down the pub of an evening (as they often did), you could be said to be asking for trouble. As the old saying goes – walls have ears – even old walls (or old ears).

As for punishment, it's somewhat interesting to consider that in the seventeenth and eighteenth centuries, the penalty for nicking say, a lace hankie, or a spoon, was exactly the same as for highway robbery or even murder. In fact, there were over a hundred and sixty offences that could leave the culprit dangling on a rope. Theft of anything over a shilling in value carried the death sentence. Not much of a deterrent there, if you think about it. If you were going to be hanged anyway, you might just as well think big.

By the Way

Just in case you were considering going into the highway robbery business yourself, it would actually be better to do it now rather than then. It was quite common for kids of thirteen – boys or girls – to be executed for the most petty of crimes (like not eating their crusts). Having said that, it would probably be better for all concerned that you don't become highwaypeople at all (the last thing I need is a cross letter from your mum or dad).

Twelve Bob Hanging

From the records of the *Western Flying Post*, 1812, comes

the story of 24 year-old James Williams who jumped out on farmer Edward Locock while he was passing through the parish of Upottery near Honiton, Devon. Locock was made to hand over a handkerchief worth one shilling (5p); a pair of gloves (also 5p); the horse's bridle valued at four shillings (20p); his saddle at five shillings (25p); an empty purse worth three pence and a couple of scraps of paper at only one penny — all in all no more than twelve shillings (60p). He was hanged at Exeter Gaol on Friday 18th April 1812.

Hang 'em All

Hanging as a punishment for practically any social naughtiness got so out of hand that, by the end of the eighteenth century, the judges were directed to send everyone they possibly could to our colonies — often a fate worse than death (still is, in my opinion). Over a thousand a year were being dispatched by the late 1700s.

This even applied to some highwaymen. If the prisoner had carried out his (or her) business without resorting to murder (violence was okay, but murder, no way), there was a pretty good chance of avoiding the old rope and being sent on a nice long ocean cruise, usually to Maryland or Virginia in America or to the hot, sweaty plantations of the West Indies and later Australia. Not only that, but many a clever (for 'clever' read 'rich') prisoner could slip the judge a handful of gold coins to escape both. Despite this, over 500 highwaymen's feet did dangle above the ground (that's 250 highwaymen, by the way)★ between 1750 and 1770. On one occasion forty were hanged in one day.

★ *Providing there weren't any with only one leg.*

Hulks Ahoy

Before actually leaving England for their foreign visit, most highwaymen could expect a spell on the disgusting, rotting hulks – those spooky, decommissioned ex-galleons parked on the wide bit of the Thames and at a few southern seaside ports (they were a bit like cars that had failed their MOT). Since 1776 they were used as temporary prisons as, at this time, most of London's prisons were only really for people waiting for their trial, for execution, or for those who owed money. The reason for this was simple. Prisons in those days were nearly all privately owned and debtors could be held there until they or their families coughed up the dosh to get 'em out. In fact, in prisons like the infamous Newgate (see page 47) or Marshalsea, whole families often stayed together in cells that were like tiny (not to mention filthy) apartments. Imagine that – your dad loses a packet down the betting shop and the whole lot of you (dog and budgie included) have to go to prison with him. Rotten deal, eh!

Rich Pickings

Transportation to foreign parts was really profitable for the ship owners who carried the convicts, as they got between £10 and £25 (about £750 and £1,875 in modern money) per person, if delivered alive and in one piece (not always the case), plus an extra fiver from the government back home. From 1788, the powers that be decided that Australia might be rather a nice place to send convicts to but the conditions were so bloomin' awful on the eight-month voyages, locked up as they were, in filthy, sweaty holds, that many perished from a whole series of fabulous diseases before even reaching their destination (where a whole lot more perished from another whole series of fabulous diseases).

By the Way

Quite a few of the transported highwaymen, who tended to be a bit smarter than the rest, escaped and set up business (robbing, of course) in their new country, instead of trying to get home. Most of those who did get back to the old country, after serving their sentence found themselves in exactly the same situation as they'd been before – broke! Most simply got out their guns, saddled up their horses, slipped on their masks and started again as if nothing had happened.

Benefit of the Clergy

There used to be a great wheeze for getting out of the most serious sentences. It was called 'Benefit of the Clergy' and it worked like this. Way back to the twelfth century any ordained person was entitled to be tried by the church court rather than the ordinary civil one – a real doddle. If found guilty he would be made to serve a much lighter sentence (hanging wasn't allowed) under the jurisdiction of the bishop. Later on, this loophole was extended to anyone who could prove ordination and this was done by a literacy test (the clergy were usually the only ones who could read anyway). The accepted test for literacy was to be able to read the penitent's prayer (nicknamed the 'neck verse'), which went:

Have Mercy on me, oh God
According to thy steadfast love;
According to thy abundant mercy
Blot out my transgressions.
Wash me thoroughly from my iniquity,
And cleanse me from my sin

Well, playmates, it doesn't take the biggest genius who ever lived to work out that, apart from the better-educated felons being highwaymen, the verse could be learned parrot fashion (let's face it, have you ever heard of a parrot being hanged?), without the guilty party being able to read at all. Believe it or not, this daft escape route was not totally abandoned until the 1800s.

Time to be Hanged

But this chapter's mostly about hanging, and this is what I am about to describe. Apart from the famous hanging places, like Tyburn or Execution Dock (for pirates) in Wapping and, of course, prisons like Newgate, many were hanged or transported (when dead) to the very place where they'd dunnit – so to speak, as a warning to any people with similar ideas. There they would dangle from gibbets in sinister iron body-shaped cages, for all to see and, as their corpses gradually decomposed and their very flesh rotted away to their bare bones, they, rather inconsiderately I think, created some of the most awful sights and pongs in history (next to my spaniel, Kevin). This treatment, by the way, was carried out particularly if they'd robbed mail carriers and the foul practice went on until 1834.

Worse still, was the description of how some of the really naughty road robbers were gibbeted alive, hung up in the metal cages where they languished in agony, covered in flies

and pecked at by crows until
dead. Anyone who tried to help
them could have expected
similar treatment. This
happened to a few
highwaymen who
hung in agony (and
with nothing to read)

FANCY A HIGHWAYMAN?

for days until, if lucky, some kindly passer-by took a pot shot
at him to put him out of his misery.

Four Ways at Once

But that still was pretty mild stuff. This is what happened if
they REALLY didn't like you. Take the case of the highly
educated and deeply refined Captain James Hind, a
highwayman who, being a Royalist, specialised in robbing
Roundheads during the English Civil War. A case of
choosing to rob the right side at the wrong time!

First of all, poor James was hanged by the neck for about
five minutes (long enough to give him a severe sore throat,
but not enough to kill him). As if that wasn't enough, he
was then castrated (the cruellest cut of all), disembowelled
and his intestines burned in front of him – WHILE STILL
ALIVE – OOOUUUCH! Finally he was beheaded (which
usually does the trick) and his body cut roughly (arms and
legs attached) into four parts, doused in preserving fluid and
then sent to four different corners of the city wall.

Here's an account from some relatives who came to visit
their recently executed family member:

'When we first came to Newgate there lay (in a little by-
place like a closet near the room where we were lodged) the
quartered bodies of three men that had been executed some
days before. The heads were ordered to be set up in some

part of the City. I saw the heads
when they were brought up to be
boiled . . . the Hangman put them
into his kettle and parboiled them with
bay salt and cummin seed [yum!], that to
keep them from putrefaction and this to
keep the fowls [birds] from seizing them.'

By the Way

The idea of cutting someone into four
parts, or indeed removing any bit of his body, was based on
the unlikely religious premise that in order to go to heaven
your body must be in one piece (what about a bishop with
a wooden leg? – I ask myself). Oddly enough, this really
used to worry the wig off a hardened criminal who, I'd have
thought, might just have reckoned he'd ruined his chances
of a halo and wings long ago.

Hanging for All

Let's get back to the actual hanging. As most highwaymen
were kept in Newgate (see page 47) we'll start from there.
On the prisoner's last night, the prison chaplain would visit
and try to extract any further gory stories or confessions –
on pain of going to hell if he didn't talk. This was a nice
sideline, as the canny old chaplains would then sell the
'Account' to the local penny broadsheets (sensationalist
papers a bit like some of ours) which would then be flogged
to the crowds lining the route to Tyburn or at the execution
itself. The justification for this blatant piece of profiteering
was that it was to show the great unwashed just how easy it
was to graduate from little crimes to great big ones. Nice to
see the clergy so in tune with their public, don't you think?

On hanging day, usually a Monday (and usually a public

holiday, called Tyburn Fair Day), the condemned men (including our heroes) would leave by the back door of Newgate in a horse-drawn cart – up to twenty at a time.

A nice touch – if the villains needed any reminding of their fate – was to pile their coffins into the following cart. Actually the coffins were for the lucky ones, for if there weren't enough to go round, it meant the others were to be gibbeted or dissected by eager medical students. In the carriage behind them would be the Sheriffs of London just to make the occasion that bit more special.

Famous highwaymen could attract anything up to 100,000 spectators and, dressed in their finest clothes, they were generally cheered all along the procession's route. It was almost a jolly occasion, a bit like a royal wedding (if you think that's a jolly occasion), with a load of street sellers providing anything from gin to sweets. It goes without saying that hanging days were like Christmas for pickpockets.

The procession soon passed the gates of St Sepulchre's Church in Newgate Street where the condemned were each given a little bunch of flowers and then it was all along the Tyburn Valley. Then onward up Heavy (now Holborn) Hill and through the Holborn tollgate which marked the boundary of the City. (The little group was now in, believe it or not, the countryside.) They'd then travel along Holborn and St Giles and round what is now New Oxford Street (then rather nasty marshland as opposed to a rather nasty shopping street). At the halfway mark the occupants were allowed a last drink (Perrier, naturellement) at a tavern called The Bowl. Here they would often get totally drunk (wouldn't you?) in order to face the ordeal ahead. The little procession would then progress along Oxford Street to 'Tyburn Tree' (what is now Marble Arch). All in all a distance of only three miles but it often took up to two hours.

Time to Talk

On reaching the gallows, the more famous highwaymen would be allowed to give a goodbye speech – sometimes up to an hour in length and often really funny. The crowd loved this and booed if the victim showed any sign of fear. Some felons attacked the actual hangman, or even the chaplain, and the crowd thought this a real hoot.

The Bitter End

Very often, as a perk of the job, the hangman was allowed to keep the deceased's clothes to wear (if they fitted) or to sell to the crowd. As the body was taken down from the scaffold, the crowd would surge forward either to touch the still warm body or to try to remove some little memento. It was thought that the 'death sweat' of a recently executed person (especially of a highwayman), contained magical medical powers, and a sick mother would fight to brush the limp hand against her face, or the faces of her kids. If a woman could not have children, the magic hand would also do the trick. If you were lucky enough to be given the skull, it could be used as a cup from which he who drank could be cured of epilepsy; and if said skull was left long enough to gather mould or moss, the scrapings were supposed to be jolly good for headaches (beats aspirin, I suppose). One beautiful woman was seen to expose her breast in front of the thousands of cheering onlookers and place the dead hand upon it. Aren't some people weird?

Almost best of all (if you're as gruesome as me) – if a hanged man's hand fell into the possession of burglars, they could dry and pickle it and use it as a candle holder. Instead of candles the actual fingers could be lit. Why bother? Because, if they entered a house carrying this weird candelabrum, the poor occupants would fall under a spell and the lads could do their work in peace.

THIEF-TAKERS

Before I tell you who and what thief-takers were, it might be an idea to drone on a bit about how the law was (or wasn't) enforced all those years ago. Right up to the late 1700s, any proper grown-up organised form of law and order in this country was resisted by the rich and powerful as they claimed (quite rightly) that it would interfere with liberty. What they really meant was that, as they were so blinking corrupt themselves, any form of law and order would, for sure, interfere with their liberty to continue the dodgy dealing they'd been getting away with for years. (Like parliamentary 'sleaze' these days!)

There were, however, parish constables (amateurs), night-watchmen (called Charlies) and beadles (parish officials) in London in those days, but they were well aware that they were unable to do a thing to stem the enormous surge of crime. The constables, for instance, were simply ordinary members of the public who, when their name came up, had to do a year's service for no money – a dangerous and thankless task (like writing these bloomin' books!). Most times these good men of London Town did their level best to get out of it, even paying others, if at all possible, to do their duty for them.

By the Way

There used to be something called the 'Tyburn ticket' in the eighteenth century: a system by which any constable, if he managed to get someone convicted and topped at the famous gallows (Tyburn), could be let off the rest of his term.

The trouble with all these systems was that they were far too local, only really operating in the little areas that they were designed to look after. A half-canny criminal only had to cross boundaries or even come in from another one (and then run away) and there was seemingly nothing that could be done about it.

Thief-takers

Thief-taking started during the reign of William and Mary (1689–1702). Some clever-clogs reckoned that the answer to all the robbery on the public thoroughfares was to set up a system of rewards to be given to anyone who could supply information that would lead to the arrest of a highwayman (in particular), or indeed any number of other criminals. In other words a tell-tale's charter. In more other words, a bit like all those crime watch programmes that we have on the telly (only with cash prizes).

How Much?

In the beginning, the bounty for a highwayman was £40 (about £3,000 now) – plus, would you believe, the poor bloke's money, weapons and even his horse (I suppose where he was going, he wouldn't need any of those). So far so good, I expect you think. Where it all went a bit wonky, was that the powers-that-be also offered a free pardon to the tale-teller, meaning that anyone who was either convicted of a crime or was just about to be, would

be let off. Now, it doesn't take Sherlock Holmes to work out that, if you were, how shall I put it, slightly not-very-honest, with a lot of not-very-honest mates, there was a good business to be made snitching on them and copping the reward. The professional thief-taker or bounty hunter was born.

It was a good system, but seriously open to corruption: just think, a private individual would not only put the word out if they had been robbed but would even employ other private individuals to track the culprit down. For this, the 'detective' would get about half of everything he managed to retrieve plus the large fee for bringing the criminal to justice. So far so good – but have you spotted the other potential scam? If you were really clever, and really, really tricksy, you could actually organise the robberies, contact the victim, return the stolen goods and then, and here's the good bit, turn in the guys you got to do it, for yet another reward – three sources of cash in one. Wicked admittedly, but nonetheless brilliant.

On 3 June 1752 a professional thief-taker, Thomas Norton, took a coach to Halfway House, between Knightsbridge and Kensington, having heard a tip-off that it was to be robbed. Sure enough, the famous highwayman William Belcher was in attendance and was arrested by Norton as they each went about their business.

Jonathan Wilde

Best, or should I say worst, of the lot was a guy called Jonathan Wilde who, on the surface, seemed a highly respectable London magistrate but underneath turned out to be a lying,

JONATHAN WILDE

cheating b . . . blackguard. First of all, he planned brilliant robberies for thieves and highwaymen throughout the land, mostly using men who'd illegally escaped from hard labour in the colonies. He would then receive anything they stole and try to sell it back to their original owners. If the thieves refused to play, or even complained, he could turn them in, which meant, when it came right down to it, that they were being blackmailed. The men he did inform on were almost always found guilty and, all-in-all, Wilde, later nicknamed the 'Thief-Taker General of Great Britain and Ireland' managed to send over sixty to their deaths on the gallows, and picked up a tidy sum in *blood money* (which is where the term came from).

Because of the number of crooks he sent to the gallows, he tried (albeit unsuccessfully) to become a Freeman of the City of London (a big deal in the olden days), and he would strut around the streets, silver-topped cane in hand, as if he owned the place. For several years highwaymen avoided London like the plague which meant, I suppose, that in a funny sort of roundabout way, he did succeed in ridding the city of a well-known scourge. Eventually, however, Jonathan Wilde took a tumble over a little piece of French lace that one of his robber chums had stolen and he (Wilde) tried to wheedle a reward from. Not much in itself, but the link that everyone suspected was made, and it was all the authorities needed to slap him in jail and eventually string him up.

His execution, when still only 43, prompted a frenzied response from the public whom he had so cynically betrayed and he was spat at and booed all the way to the gallows.

THE BEGINNING OF
THE END

Henry Fielding (1707–1754) was the famous novelist and playwright who wrote the rather rude (but jolly funny) book *Tom Jones* and was, to most people, an all round good egg. He was made a magistrate in Westminster and moved into the now very trendy Bow Street, Covent Garden (in central London) to run his office from home. To tell the truth, the only reason he took the job was not for any do-gooding motive but because he was a bit short of ready cash. But old Henry had been casually observing the rapid rise in robbery for years and how the private thief-takers had got a stranglehold on all the capturing and rewarding side of the business. Sure, said Henry, you could continue upping the rewards for the arrest of villains, but that would simply be doling out cash to those thieving thief-takers (these guys were even up to tempting innocent youngsters to commit crimes simply so they could nick 'em and pocket the rewards).

Fielding also despaired of the decrepit Charlies, the rickety old watchmen mentioned on page 44, not to mention the unpaid parish constables (also see page 62) who were only really interested in passing the job on to some other poor sucker. As for executions or public hangings, he reckoned that although, admittedly, they weren't that brilliant for highwaymen (even though they mostly seemed to make a joke of it) they had simply become a fab day out for all the family – an entertainment for the masses – a theme park with hanging (and worse) as the main attraction. Despite the number of necks the authorities stretched, they seemed to be going nowhere towards putting off others. He was well aware that although a huge number of poor devils went rumbling past his place in the tumbrils on their merry way to Tyburn and death, they were few in comparison to the hundreds of others that were *not* (and who should have been).

Fielding decided that the only answer was to make the actual doing of the crimes less easy and the only way to do that was to start a proper Police Force (even if he didn't know what the words meant). Old Fielding scoffed at those who said it would take away an Englishman's freedom, claiming, quite rightly that they'd only lose it if they actually did something wrong.

The first step was to get the pawnbrokers (the legal receivers of second-hand goods) on his side by asking them nicely to check the lists of stolen items, and report anything dodgy that was offered to them. Fielding then put an ad in the papers (or penny broadsheets) offering to interview anyone who'd been robbed. Would you believe it, nobody had ever thought of that before.

Mr Fielding's People

Fielding met a chap called Welch who'd been made head of the Holborn non-paid constables and was apparently an honest man (rare in those days). Together they formed the first sort of CID (Criminal Investigation Department) using six of his most trustworthy constables as investigators. Still no pay involved but, like the thief-takers, they could receive decent rewards for anyone they caught.

But if you ever go thinking London's less than safe now than ever before, it was a blinking nightmare (literally) for the night-time traveller in 1750 – there were highwaymen or footpads lurking in practically every shadow and behind every tree. As Horace Walpole, another famous writer, wrote: 'Robbing is the only thing that goes on with any vivacity' and that 'going to a friend's house in London is as dangerous as going to the relief of Gibraltar'*. On another occasion he said 'one is forced to travel even at noon as if one is going to battle'. It has to be said that no crime wave in history compared remotely with the one in England in the mid eighteenth century and, if you don't believe me, even the King was held up by a highwayman in his own back yard at Kensington Palace. Brilliant!

Anyway, these slightly wet-behind-the-ears policemen, nicknamed Mr Fielding's People, did well at first, but it was still a drop (or drip) in the ocean compared to all the stuff which was still going on. Too many highwaymen were getting away scot-free and if something wasn't done soon, Fielding ranted, every street in London and all the roads leading to and from it would be impassable – and impossible.

But by now Henry was old, sick and in a wheelchair so he asked the government if his half-brother John could share the job with him. A fine pair they made: Henry was dying and his half brother (to be nicknamed the 'Blind Beak') was blind (not even half blind). John

* *Big news story of the time. In 1704, during the War of the Spanish Succession, Gibraltar was captured by English and Dutch forces.*

must have looked fairly menacing when suspects appeared before him in court as he wore a black strip of cloth round his sightless eyes.

By the Way
Blind John's hearing was so sharpened by the fact that he couldn't see, that it was alleged that he could distinguish the voices of over three thousand different thieves.

A Proper Plan
The minister in charge of crime and all that sort of thing, the Duke of Newcastle, not only agreed with the Fieldings' concern but asked the two bro's to draw up a suitable plan to solve it. The first thing they did was to turn Henry's house into a twenty-four-hour manned 'nick' – sorry – police station, which, amazingly, it still is, although the present building (built in 1879) is on the other side of the road. The Fieldings then organised to have two men always on call (and on horses) ready to go whenever it was, to whatever it was and wherever it was . . . in the country, and to keep a register of all the crimes and of all the people that just might have done 'em. Then, as now, it was usually just a case of pairing them up. All in all it was to cost £600 a year, a lot of money in those days but, compared to the amount of rewards that were currently being dished out to those pesky thief-takers, it was peanuts.

Bow Street Runners
Unfortunately, the 'Bow Street Runners', as they were now officially called, were viewed at first in exactly the same light as the thief-takers by the general public, but no one could deny the success they were beginning to have (the number of big crimes in London having dropped like a stone). There

was still a long way to go, however, for highway robberies outside the city were almost as bad as ever. John Fielding reckoned that the general public weren't on the ball enough and in 1755 issued a 'Plan for Preventing Robberies within Twenty Miles of London' in which he begged the public to help in any way they knew how and to let his lads know of crimes as soon as they'd happened.

BOW STREET RUNNER

Costly Business

But poor blind John had more things to worry about. The Home Office was slow in paying him back the money he was lashing out on pursuing highwaymen. It was an expensive business to be sure : 'Waylaying a highwayman at a turnpike, 5s,' 'Pursuing a highwayman near Hackney, 17s 6d,' 'Sitting in a hospital with a wounded highwayman until fit to be examined £1 11s 6d' etc. etc.

Things continued to get worse, so in 1761, John put forward another far-reaching plan. The Government rejected most of it, admittedly, but agreed to fund a civilian Horse Patrol of ten men (and presumably ten horses) – five experienced, five not. The effects were immediate and by the spring of 1764 all the roads leading out of London had been made safe. Too blinking safe! The Government, seeing the problem was now as good as over, decided to abandon the Horse Patrol. And guess what? Within a few weeks those wily old robbers were all back and at it again.

Back Again

The government reluctantly coughed up again, and again the highwaymen high-tailed it back to where they came from. Unbelievably, shortly after, it was abandoned again – and this time for ages. By the 1770s the roads were worse than ever before, with just about everyone, lord or lout, lady or lass being held up on the roads leaving London as a matter of course – of course!

Postscript

London had to wait until 1805 for a regular Horse Patrol to be reinstated and that was the beginning of a rather swift end for the highwaymen of England.

THE BEST OF THE BUNCH

Claude Duval – The Most Charming

Miller's son Claude Duval, was born in France (Normandy to be precise) in 1643 and, when a teenager, moved to Paris where he met lots of Royalist Englishmen on the run from that rotten Roundhead Oliver Cromwell. Claude came to England as a servant to the Duke of Richmond (it was real flash in those days to have French staff) but, being an adventurous sort of lad, he found this a bit boring so decided on a career of robbing people. He must have been quite good because he reached the top of the wanted list (the highwaymen's hit parade) by 1668.

Claude Duval had gained a massive reputation with the general public, especially the ladies, as he was ever so handsome, witty and terribly flirty (and all that with a French accent). He was *so* popular with his female fans, in fact, that it became quite a status symbol to get yourself held up by him.

On one occasion he heard that there'd be a coach crossing Hounslow Heath carrying a titled gent, his wife and, more to the point, £400 pounds hard cash (around £29,000 in today's money). The lady, seeing the highwayman approaching, knew who he was and, being not the least bit afraid, pulled out her flageolet (a little recorder) and began to play sweetly. Duval promptly whipped out *his* (flageolet) and played sweetly back. The charming highwayman then complemented the knight on how pretty his missus was and how well she played. Pushing his luck, he asked hubby if she danced as well as she tootled. The knight, realising Duval was a true gentleman (who had a blinking great pistol in his hand), allowed the lady to dance with the robber in the moonlight. Duval, of course, danced beautifully and returned the lady flushed and swooning to her carriage.

He then almost casually reminded the knight that the whole purpose of the exercise was cash – his cash! 'I'll tell you what', he laughed, 'why not regard it as payment for the entertainment'. The knight thought this totally reasonable and was about to hand over the four hundred quid when Duval said he would only take a hundred because of his wife's charming performance.

As the knight had thought – a true gent.

End of the Road

Duval was eventually picked up, armed to the teeth and drunk as a skunk, in a tavern in London. He was sentenced to death and, though countless well-connected people tried desperately to get him off, he was hanged at Tyburn in 1670 when still only 27 years of age.

The poor ex-highwayman was taken to lie 'in state' at the notorious Tangier Tavern at St Giles (in London) and it is no exaggeration to say that there was a procession of up-market dames wearing masks (so's not to be recognised) who stopped to weep over his body, it was surrounded by candles and watched over by eight tall men in black cloaks – to prevent the ladies from throwing themselves on the corpse. This poem was later engraved on his gravestone:

> Here lies Du Vall; Reader, if Male thou art,
> Look to thy purse; if Female, to thy heart.
> Much havoc has he made of both; for all
> Men he made stand, and women he made fall.
> The second Conqueror of the Norman race*,
> Knights to his arms did yield, and Ladies to his face.
> Old Tyburn's glory; England's illustrious thief,
> Du Vall, the Ladies' joy; Du Vall, the Ladies' grief.

* *William was the first.*

Dick Turpin – The Most Notorious

Just mention highwaymen, and everyone thinks of Dick Turpin. He's generally thought of as a brave, romantic, swashbuckling figure much like Robin Hood. But, like Robin Hood (who probably didn't even have the good sense to exist) a lot of the stories are exaggerated and even out and out porkies. For instance, he never had a horse called Black Bess and never did that famous ride from London to York in one go – so there!

In fact, instead of being the gallant handsome gentleman of the road, it is reported that he was quite a nasty piece of work, and ugly to boot. Nasty and ugly OK, but nonetheless brave. The 'King of the Road', as he was nicknamed, was born in 1705 at Hempstead, Essex, the son of an innkeeper, and started his working life as a trainee butcher in Whitechapel, London. While running his own shop he discovered that there was much more money to be made from nicking the actual animals that he was to chop up and sell. But he was soon found out and had to get out of town and back to Essex pretty smartish. We next hear of him as a smuggler in Canvey Island – well, not actually a smuggler, but someone who rather cunningly held up smugglers after they'd done all the hard work. Turpin did this by pretending to be a revenue officer, but again was soon found out and had once more to move on rather quicker than he would perhaps have chosen. It was then on to deer rustling with the infamous Essex Gang who supplemented their income with a bit of local house-breaking.

The Essex Gang was a nasty bunch to be sure, robbing and raping all over the Epping Forest area, and soon there was a reward of a hundred guineas on each of their heads. But our Dick got fed up with group crime and wanted to go it alone, which he did, in 1735, aged 30, when he started out as a solo highwayman. Within two years he was by far the most famous throughout the length and breadth of England and almost a folk hero in his native Essex.

Later, by the way, he specialised in the common land between Barnes and Wandsworth in London (now the common haunt of dastardly estate agents and cowboy builders). He was easily recognisable for his pale, pockmarked, broad face and intense staring eyes.

Dick teamed up for a while with a fellow robber Tom King, and they lived (some of the time with Mrs Turpin) in a cave in the middle of Epping Forest. There they could hide for weeks on end even though they had their horses with them and they were close to two roads (which they watched through peep-holes ever seeking potential victims).

What made Turpin famous was his staggering brutality, which was unusual among the elite of the profession. Unlike his fellow highwaymen he had no problem with hurting and killing. Sure, most highwaymen threatened – but few actually did what they said they were going to do. Dick's reasoning was simple, however. After all, he must have thought, if I'm going to get hanged for robbery anyway I might just as well get rid of the witnesses. It sort of worked, as for ages he remained free, – nobody daring to risk collecting the reward for telling on him.

His first murder victim was one of the forest keepers who followed him to his secret hidey-hole. The next was his own partner, Tom King, whom he rather carelessly shot by mistake (whoops!) while aiming at a Bow Street Runner who'd recognised them (pistols in those days left a lot to be desired accuracy-wise). In a weird fit of revenge for the tragic mistake (which was nobody's fault but his own) Turpin went on an orgy of robbing, holding up someone every single day for the next month or so*. Turpin eventually turned his back on highway robbery when the amount of money on his head reached £200 (nearly £14,000 in today's money). But our Dick simply couldn't go straight and a year later he was caught, accused of horse-stealing and sentenced to hang.

Dick Turpin, by the way, was most jolly and sociable while waiting in prison for his big day, for he was convinced it would never happen. But happen it did – on April 7, 1739. The most famous of all highwaymen died bravely, confessing in the end to countless robberies, and apologising

---

* It was someone different every day, by the way, otherwise the person would have got very fed up.

only for killing the bloke who'd stumbled on his hideout in the forest. He then chucked himself into the air with a chuckle and died dangling five minutes later. He was still only 34 years old.

By the Way

If you want to see where Dick drank, go to the Spaniards Inn on Hampstead Heath. If you want to see his prison cell, visit the Castle Museum in York.

John Cottington (alias 'Mulled Sack' after his favourite drink) – The Bravest

John Cottington had a difficult start in life. His dad, a haberdasher, died a hopeless drunk, leaving little John, his mother and his eighteen brothers and sisters destitute (not much time for haberdashery, I'd have thought). John's first proper job was working for five women in the head-shaving business (wigs were so sweaty), but that ended when they were all sent to the pillory or deported for various petty crimes. So from an early age the lad was out on the streets stealing anything that might be turned into money to buy food. A true Londoner, and yet another staunch follower of the King, he chose carefully whom he robbed, never touching anyone loyal to the royals. Having been at it since childhood he became a pro, even carrying chain-cutting scissors (specially made for him) to sever necklaces, watch-chains, bracelets and of course purses from

THAT'LL BE A WEIGHT OFF YOUR MIND SIR!

77

their unsuspecting owners. One of his most famous prey was Oliver Cromwell himself, which was about the worst career move he could make as it nearly got him hanged.

After this incident, he decided to pack up the small stuff and become a proper highwayman, choosing Hounslow Heath as his area of operations. He teamed up with an ex-soldier Tom Cheyney, but Cheyney was hurt seriously in a hold-up that went rather wrong. They bravely, if somewhat stupidly, took on a whole troop of soldiers. So seriously hurt was Tom, in fact, that the powers that be had to hurry up his trial and execution in case he died first. Poor Tom was found guilty at lunchtime and hanged only a few hours later that afternoon, probably an all-time Guinness world record.

Mulled Sack was one of the most successful of all highwaymen, once robbing a heavily protected army pay-wagon of £4,000 (nearly £250,000 these days) in hard cash. Be that as it may, he, just like his partner, was caught and hanged at Smithfield in 1656 – still a relatively young man.

Lady Katherine Ferrers – The Prettiest

Lady Katherine Ferrers, like her male counterparts in the highway robbery business, came from the other side of society (and blanket) – the top drawer in fact. At sixteen she had married the extremely rich Lord Ferrers and was a beautiful and dutiful wife in their massive mansion just outside London (Hemel Hempstead) until she decided it was all too terribly tedious. Unfortunately, they didn't have the Women's Institute, coffee mornings or charity shops in those days, so she had to find something else constructive to do with her time. So saying, our Kath would wait till the end of the evening and, having kissed her old hubby goodnight (they always had separate bedrooms in those days), she'd dress up in her hidden highwayman's outfit, take

a secret passage out of the house and rob coaches as they came and went from the city. Obviously Mrs Ferrers wasn't in it for the money – simply for the buzz.

Lady Katherine did this until eventually she was wounded in a shootout during a hold-up and, so legend has it, bled to death halfway up the stairs, having staggered all the way home. (A jolly good case for bungalows, I'd have said.) She was still only 22 years old, poor dear.

Zachary Howard – the Cheekiest

Yet another Cavalier highwayman was Captain Zachary Howard, who was so loyal to Charles I that he mortgaged his extremely valuable property in Wales to raise an army to fight for him. When the king lost his head, Zachary lost his home and lands and flew (well, sailed) to France, only to return to Scotland with Charles I's lad, Charles II, who was trying to get his dad's country back. Unfortunately, there was by then rather a lot of money on offer for Zach's capture and the only real future for him was as a highwayman. It must be said in his defence, however, that he only robbed those who were politically opposed to the king.

His jaunts were to go down in history for their daring and downright, barefaced nerve. On one occasion he halted a well-known Parliamentarian (Roundhead) who was travelling with a servant. Highwayman Howard was told in no uncertain terms to – how shall I put it – 'go away', but he promptly robbed his victim of a diamond ring and all the gold he was carrying. Laughing fit to bust, he then set the gent on his servant's horse, facing its backside, and tied the servant back to back with his master, facing the horse's head. A sharp slap on the beast's rump and it was in this predicament that master and servant eventually trotted into the next town.

Before long there was the unheard-of reward of 500 Roundhead pounds on Zachary Howard's head but, undeterred, the brave captain decided after a short 'rest' in Ireland to have a personal go at his worstest enemy, Oliver Cromwell, the Lord Protector (boss) of All England. So saying, he contrived to stay (in disguise) at the same inn in Chester as the big man himself. The story goes that Howard soon made friends with the rebel leader and was invited to his rooms for prayers. I think I'd have preferred a bedtime drink, and so would Howard, I should imagine, for he promptly pulled out his pistol, tied old Ollie up, took all his money and then as an afterthought, picked up the nearly full chamber-pot (no lavs in those days) and crowned Cromwell 'in the manner he deserved'.

Like so many good stories there's a bit of a sad end to this one. When Howard was eventually caught in 1652, the still furious Cromwell came to see him at

Maidstone Gaol and personally saw to his execution, just as he had King Charles's three years earlier.

William Davis (The Golden Farmer) – the Most Devious

Wealthy farmer, pillar of respectable society, regular churchgoer, father of eighteen – these aren't qualities you instantly connect with a life of robbery on the open road. But William Davis was all of these things, and got away with being a part-time robber for over forty years, even in broad daylight, by his mastery of the art of disguise. Many of his victims, usually cattlemen on their way home from market with their gold coins jingling in their pockets, were chaps that knew him pretty well in everyday life. On one occasion, after he had just been visited by his landlord who'd collected his annual rent, he donned a disguise and followed him up the road. The landlord not knowing him from Adam, claimed, on being held up, that he only had a few pence on him. Davis knew better and took his seventy guineas rent back.

When he was eventually shot and captured the whole neighbourhood was in uproar, as he had been someone they had all looked up to. And look up to him they still did, for his body, after being hanged, was left to rot in chains on Bagshot Heath in Surrey, near where he'd farmed for years.

THE END OF THE ROAD

By the end of the eighteenth century things were getting
pretty tough for your average hardworking highwayman. For
a start, for some time he'd had to contend with the reward
system, whereby any little underworld sneak could whisper a
name to any Bow Street Runner or thief-taker and make a
nice little pile. Then there was the onset of better roads,
which meant that coaches seldom went as slow or broke
down – they often just charged past the poor chilly
highwayman who'd been hanging about for ages. Better
roads also meant more traffic, which instead of providing
more business, actually annoyed highwaymen a lot. Robbing
defenceless coaches depended on the roads being deserted.
I mean, imagine being a highwayman these days. You'd have
to do all your robbing at the service stations (which are
daylight robbery anyway).

On top of all that, the poor chaps had to contend with
all those toll house keepers who were beginning to get
chummy with the Bow Street Runners, passing on
information gleaned from the travellers. The net was
tightening like a . . . tight net!

Don't Fence me in

But worse still, was the dratted enclosure system, which was
stitching England up good and proper. Instead of the wide
open spaces to escape over, highwaymen had to run in and
out and round about a labyrinth of hedgerows and fences
enclosing smaller and smaller fields. Hardly any horses, by
the way, had been taught to jump over things in those days★,
so the poor old highwayman, if cornered, found himself

★ *At least that meant they didn't have to put up with show-jumping.*

having to get off and walk his dozy dobbin round the obstacle if he wanted to scarper.

No Room in the Inn

The highwayman was becoming a social leper. Even finding somewhere to rest for the night to have a drink and something to eat (and pore over the loot) was becoming tricky. There were fewer and fewer licences dished out to landlords who were known to offer highwaymen hospitality (and the knowing wink).

Nothing to Steal

But difficult as all this was making it for the highwayman to go about his everyday stealing, he still worked on the assumption that there was still something to steal out there on the open roads. This wasn't always true. It had taken a long time, but the early banks had eventually cottoned on to the huge amounts of cash their clients, especially animal traders, were 'losing' on their way home from the London markets, and had started a system by which the cash could be paid into accounts in the City – the beginning of proper banking. Eventually even the deals themselves were done with notes of credit (early cheques) which was all terrible news for the poor, patient highwayman waiting in the shadows for cash on delivery.

The gradual establishment of banks was to really put the kybosh on things. By the end of the century it was mostly boring old cheques and bills of sale being carried in place of the wonderfully untraceable silver and gold. Cheques, as you might imagine, weren't much use if you didn't have a bank account – and highwaymen generally didn't.

Blood Money for All

When the general public got in on the act and realised that they could receive rewards for informing on highwaymen, the end finally loomed into view. Suddenly our poor hero found himself with no friends, nowhere to rob, nothing to steal and nowhere to go (after not having done it).

By 1750 it was more or less all over and so, my incredibly patient readers, is this book.

HIGHWAYMAN-SPEAK

Robbers and highwaymen had a language all of their own and many of the expressions have survived to this day. All the following words would have been common talk amongst highwaymen of the seventeenth and eighteenth centuries.

Adam's ale: *Water (still in use)*

autem-mort: *A married woman*

back'd: *Dead*

bandittis: *Highwaymen*

belly-cheat: *An apron*

bene-cove: *A good man*

bene-darkmans: *Goodnight*

bilk the rattling cove: *To cheat a coachman (Bilk is still used by cab drivers)*

binged awast in the darkness: *Fled by night*

bingo: *Brandy*

bit: *To thieve*

bingo-boy: *A lover of strong drink*

bite the bill from the cull: *Steal a sword from a gentleman's side*

bite the biter: *Rob another thief*

black-spy: *A real nasty bloke*

bleed freely: *Easily robbed*

bluffer: *An innkeeper*

caffin: *Cheese*

darbies: *Prison fetter, handcuffs or shackles (still in use)*

darkmans: *The night*

dim mort: *A babe*

duds: *Clothes (still in use)*

earnes: *Share of the loot*

equipped: *Rich*

fencing-cully: *A receiver of stolen goods*

fogus: *Tobacco*

gelt: *Money (still in use)*

gentry-cove: *A Gentleman*

gentry-mort: *A Gentlewoman*

glaziers: *Eyes*

grinders: *Teeth*

hamlet: *A High Constable*

hick: *A rather thick country man (still in use)*

joseph: *A coat (maybe from Joseph's coat of many colours)*

kicks: *Trousers*

kinchen: *Children*

knight of the road: *A top highwayman*

lobkin: *A lodging house*

lowpad: *The lowest form of thief*

lurries: *Easily removable jewellery*

moon-curser: *Someone who robs only by moonlight*

nab: *A hat*

nim-glimmer: *A doctor or surgeon*

nubbing-cheat: *The gallows*

nubbin-cove: *A hangman*

nubbing-ken: *A court, or place for a trial*

nut-cracker: *The pillory*

ogles: *Eyes (still in use)*

Paddington Fair: *Tyburn*

prance: *A horse*

rattler: *A coach*

rattler-cove: *A coachman*

rum-ogles: *Charming eyes (referring to women)*

sack: *A pocket*

shappo (from the French chapeau): *A very expensive hat*

squeek: *A victim yelling for help*

tatler: *A watch*

tip: *To help a comrade in trouble*

togemans: *A cloak or coat*

velvet: *A tongue*

whiddle: *One who talks too much and gives away secrets*

xantippe: *A nagging woman*

yarum: *Milk*

yellow boy: *Gold*

THE SHORT AND
BLOODY
HISTORY
OF

All aboard, Landlubbers!

PIRATES

John Farman

Have you ever wondered why pirates wore gold earrings, or where the saying 'sick as a parrot' came from? And do you know who the cruellest pirate in history was?
John Farman's got all the answers, so come aboard for his short and bloody history of the day-to-day life of pirates!

£2.99   0 09 940709 4

THE SHORT AND
BLOODY
HISTORY
OF

Call me Inspector!

SPIES

John Farman

Psst! Do you know how to make invisible
ink or send a coded message? And have
you heard about the pope who was a spy?
John Farman's been doing some spying of his
own and has uncovered all the answers in this
fantastic book. But beware, this message will
self-destruct in five seconds!

£2.99   0 09 940715 9

THE SHORT AND
BLOODY
HISTORY
OF

Fancy a joust?

KNIGHTS

John Farman

Have you ever wondered how knights managed to walk, let alone fight, covered from head to foot in metal? And have you heard about the knights who became addicted to jousting? Or the one who was rescued by a monkey? It's all in John Farman's brilliant book. So arm yourself for a fact attack!

£2.99   0 09 940712

THE VERY BLOODY HISTORY of BRITAIN

WITHOUT THE BORING BITS

PART 1

&

THE VERY BLOODY HISTORY of BRITAIN

1945 TO NOW

AND STILL NOT BORING!

Warning!!!
These books could change your ideas about history for ever!

By John Farman

Do you know…
WHO planned the first Channel tunnel?
WHEN 10 Downing Street was built?
WHY there were vampires in Britain?

Bizarre, barmy and almost beyond belief, John Farman's **THE VERY BLOODY HISTORY** books make boring history lessons a thing of the – er – past.

John Farman
THE VERY BLOODY HISTORY OF BRITAIN PART 1
Red Fox paperback £3.99 ISBN 0 09 984010 3

THE VERY BLOODY HISTORY OF BRITAIN - 1945 to now
Red Fox paperback £3.99 ISBN 0 09 937221 5

The Very Bloody History of London

By John Farman

WITHOUT THE BORING BITS

When a man is tired of London, he is tired of life... Samuel Johnson

Let John Farman, author of the mega-bestselling title *The Very Bloody History of Britain,* guide you round one of the world's most famous cities, London. Packed with a multitude of facts to entertain and amaze you, *The Very Bloody History of London* will take you on a tour you will never forget. Sometimes grisly, but always fascinating, this is history as it should be — loads of fun!

John Farman
THE VERY BLOODY HISTORY OF LONDON
Red Fox paperback, £3.99, ISBN 0 09 940412 5